Back Stabbers

She Was My Best Friend

By Robin

ROBIN

This is a work of fiction. All of the characters, organizations, and events portrayed in this novel are either a product of the author's imagination or are used fictitiously. Any resemblance to actual persons, living or dead, is purely coincidental.

'Sometimes the person you'd take a bullet for is the person behind the trigger.'

ROBIN

"They smile in your face, and the whole time they want to take your place. Them Backstabbers."

Lonely

Shanay

Sitting at the dinner table with my husband was always brutal for me. Five years of marriage and we still weren't happy with each other. We had our good times, outside the home. But when we were home, things were sad and depressing. I met Dominic, also known as Dom, in my second year of college at USC. He swept me off my feet with his handsomeness and charming ways. He was a smooth black brother, with a career as a millionaire real estate company owner. He worked long hours in his office and I worked long hours as a stockbroker. But money never made up for what was going on in our bedroom.

As time went by, I realized he was a sex maniac and I couldn't keep up with his needs. Working twelve hours a day, I didn't feel like having sex. Dom eventually got tired of it, and he cheated on me a couple times. But he promised he would never cheat again, but now I could tell he was back bored with what we had. I'd always been there for him mentally and financially, but I never satisfied him in the bedroom, and he was sick of only satisfying me.

"Do you want any more wine?" I asked Dom as I sat across the table gazing at him. I still looked at him like he was the sexiest man on earth, and he was.

"Nah, I'm straight…" he answered in a nonchalant tone, not taking his eyes off his phone as he stuffed his face with steak. I hated when Dom tended to his phone while I was trying to have a nice dinner with him. It had been going on for weeks and I was sick of it.

"I see that phone is more important than your wife trying to get her husband's attention," I shot at him, causing him to look up. Here I was sitting at the table in black lingerie with my titties spilling out my lace bra, and he was glued to his phone like I wasn't even here. He probably wished he was dining alone.

"Actually, it is since you want to know so bad. I just closed on a million dollar house, so yes, it is…"

I knew he was lying. I saw the smirk on his face as he typed and read his messages. I was foolish to think he was telling the truth. But I went along with it so I could enjoy my night.

"Well, congratulations," I said in a dry tone as I sipped my red wine.

After Dom scarfed down his meal, he wiped his mouth with a napkin and stood up.

"I have to go back down to the office to meet a client to sign papers."

"Papers? It's almost ten o'clock. I thought we were spending time together tonight?" I whined as I stood up from the table and sashayed over to him. I wrapped my arms around his waist.

"Yes, papers, babe. I promise I'll be back in two hours. Wait up for me." He kissed me and rushed out the house.

As I heard the engine of his Lamborghini roaring, I sipped my wine and went into deep thought. I could be a bitch of a wife and follow him to his office or wherever he was really going, but I didn't want to find anything that would break my heart. The first time I found him out cheating, it almost turned deadly between me and the woman. She had been pleasing my man for a year while I sat home and wondered what was wrong with me. I tried so hard to please Dominic even when it hurt, but he didn't seem interested in me. I needed a sign that I didn't have to look for to know why my husband was always running from me and how I could change it yet again…

Satisfied

Dom

Every time my wife was ready to have sex, I felt like I wanted to run away. Having sex with her was so frustrating, I couldn't take it. But I loved her. She was everything a man dreamed of, but she had changed so drastically since we got married. She used to be thick. She had wide hips, a fat ass, and her pussy was so fat and wet, I could swim in it. But her insecurities caused her to drop fifty pounds… in all the right places. Now she was stiff and skinny. She had problems with depression so I never bothered to confront her about her weight. But it was affecting us in the bedroom.

Shanay got lazy when it came to giving head, and now everything hurt when I tried to lay it on her. That's why I always found myself at the strip club at the end of the night. It wasn't any strip club though. This nude bar was for the rich and had top of the line females dancing around and serving customers with the best happy endings they could pay for. I found myself lusting on a big booty stripper chick named Monee.

Monee was a bad light skin woman and thick in the places my wife wasn't anymore. She sucked my dick so good and took my dick so deep, I always came crawling back. All she needed was one grand at the door and I had her for five hours. She'd start at the club and end in a high-priced hotel. I always had to fuck and dash though. I couldn't spend a night with her, I had to always head back home and give Shanay the boring sex she liked, and I wasn't paying Monee no more than her minimum.

I parked my Lamborghini truck in the back of the club and walked to the iron door. They saw me on the camera and opened the door. I was a VIP, so I slid the bouncer a thousand dollars cash and he let me in.

"Who you here to see?" the bouncer asked.

"Monee."

He walked me over to her private room and let me in. The room I walked into was dark with black lights glowing. It was a large sized room with a bar and DJ. It always reminded me of a bachelor pad or living room. The building was originally an office space, but the club owner bought it out and called it *The Private Room.*

I spotted Monee spinning around the pole as "Lamb Talk" by Quavo played throughout the room. The DJ saw me walk in and turned the music low. Monee was wearing a silver bikini that was glowing under the black light. She was baaaddd and worth every penny. I met her the first time I was invited to the club by my boy Jay for his bachelor party. It was only supposed to be a one-time thing, but I'd been splurging on Monee for the last year. She was like a therapist to me, but with a little extra action. I could talk to her about my problems and then she would suck my soul from my body. *How could a man not want that?*

"Hey, baby, I wasn't expecting to see you this soon. We were just texting an hour ago," Monee said as she slid down the pole.

I walked over to the white leather love seat and slid off my bomber jacket. Monee sashayed over to me in her clear, six-inch platform heels. I bit down on my bottom lip as I watched her body jiggle naturally as she made her way to me. She sat on my lap and straddled her legs on me. She started rotating her hips to the beat as she smiled at me.

"I just can't stand when she wants sex. I wish she was the old her," I blurted out and said to her.

"I thought you said you were going to counseling again and talk about it?" she asked. She knew everything I was going through. I know it sounded like a bitch move to confide in another woman. But Shanay just seemed to not have gotten it. I needed advice from another woman to understand the woman in my life.

"We are. But I don't want to hurt her feelings," I admitted.

"Look, boo. If you want your relationship to work, you have to let her know what's bothering you. I'm sure she will understand where you are coming from. She better get in there and watch some porn and get her groove back. Because I have no problem keeping you as a client and pleasing you. Hell, I'll be your girl if you want me to. But I know you love her." She stood up from my lap and picked up a bottle of Hennessy. She poured me a shot and her.

"I love her a lot but it's something about you that I'm addicted to." I took my first shot of Hennessey.

After three shots, a blunt, and watching Monee pop her ass on the pole to trap music, I was ready for my happy ending. Monee crawled over to me and took my stiff ten inches out my slightly sagging, expensive jeans.

I was a corporate man, but I was from the hood. One of the ones that made it out and actually did something other than sports or rap music. So I still dressed urban, sagged my pants, and talked the lingo. I loved ratchet women like Monee. Shit, Shanay was hood too. She was from Compton, while I was from Oakland. We all were hood and rich.

Monee slid my aching arousal in her wet mouth and started swirling her tongue around my tip while she massaged my balls. I laid my head back and let her work her magic. As she sucked on my dick and paid extra attention to my balls, I thought about how my wife was probably at home, wondering how she could fix things. I felt bad that I had to go out and find what she was lacking in, but seeing Monee was becoming an addiction. I knew I could fix things at home but running to Monee was so much easier for me. I was always a coward when it came to women. Mama taught me to not break hearts while I continued to watch her be heartbroken by my dad. I figured secrets would keep my woman happy until she found out, just like my dad did my mother. I knew I needed to change, but when I was going to change was all a mystery.

I snapped out my thoughts when I felt Monee sliding a condom on my dick. I opened my eyes and she was still on her knees.

"I figured we can finish the night here instead of a hotel. I have another client after you since you came here so early," Monee stated as she stood up.

That was cool with me. I promised Shanay I would be home tonight to give her some lovin'.

Monee sat on my dick and went to work. She was moaning loud and squirting all over me. I had to take my pants completely off so I wouldn't have to leave in my draws. She had never squirted or moaned as loud as she did tonight. She was feeling it and calling me daddy. She had a nigga turned on more than she ever did. I didn't even get to put her in any more positions. Monee rode my dick until it went soft.

"Damn, that was bomb. I'm not going to have any energy for my next customer. I wish I could call it a night," Monee said as she stood up and slid back on her thong.

"Well, if you not calling it a night, you might wanna wash all a nigga juice off you and yours. You were squirting all over my dick." I laughed and started wiping myself with my shirt. I was leaving in my jacket, a tank top and jeans. This girl had done a number on me.

"Ha ha, I usually try not to cum but tonight was different."

"Definitely a different night." I reached in my pocket and threw her something extra.

"Thank you, Dom. You always look out. I'll see you in a couple days."

After giving her a hug, I dashed out the building. I stopped at my office and took a quick shower in my personal bathroom and then I headed home. When I got there, Shanay was sleep. She was no longer in her lingerie and was now in a nightgown. I slipped out my clothes and got in bed with her. She didn't move when I wrapped my arms around her so I fell asleep pleased that I didn't have to fight with her about sex…

Laid it on Me

Monee

Two days later…

I sat in front of my best friend's job, waiting for her to come out so we could head to lunch. It was my day off, so I wanted to get into something normal. I had already spent my morning shopping, now I was ready to eat. Although I made money as an escort and private stripper, my clients always had me stressed out with all their problems and sexual demands, especially my client Dom. He was something serious that I enjoyed being with, but he was married and had a lot of issues emotionally. He went from seeing me once a month to three times a week. His sex was great, and his pay was even better, but I was starting to catch damn feelings, something I never did. He was one of my sexiest clients and he was the same age as me. I felt bad when I had to charge him, and I felt for his situation, but I was close to being a damn homewrecker. I was tired of stripping and letting men control me with money. I wanted something true and honest, and I kind of saw it in Dom.

I snapped out my thoughts when I saw my best friend walking out her job. She was wearing a burgundy business pantsuit with matching heels and Chanel purse. Her long, jet-black hair flowed as she walked. Shanay used to be thick as a Snicker, but decided to lose fifty pounds, now she looked like a Victoria's Secret model. I thought she looked great, but I'd never lose fifty pounds, I enjoyed being super thick and fine. She threw on her Gucci shades and walked over to my Ferrari with a huge smile. She hadn't seen my new ride yet so I knew that was why she was cheesing.

"Oh my god, bitch, you didn't tell me you got a new car!" Shanay shouted as she got into my car.

"I wanted to surprise you. I just got it this morning. It was imported in from the UK. Everything in this bitch is custom."

"That's what I'm talking about. I haven't had any time to spend any money. All I've been doing is working," Shanay said as she slid off her expensive heels.

"Well, you better splurge. You and your man got money, and you still riding around in that old ass Audi." I laughed a little.

"Girl, who you telling? He just bought a damn Lamborghini truck and has plenty of cars. I took a Lyft today, I need new tires. I would have drove one of his cars if we weren't having lunch today." She shrugged her shoulders.

"Well, I'ma need you to stop living like you are middle class and boss up. But let's go get some food, I'm starving."

I drove out the parking lot and found the freeway. I did 95mph on the freeway listening to Lil Wayne's *Carter V*. Me and Shanay looked like movie stars as I weaved in and out of traffic. She had the blunt going and I definitely was ready to get high before eating.

I made it to Benihanas in ten minutes from Santa Monica. We finished up the blunt, sprayed some perfume and headed inside. As we watched them cook our food, we had shots of Saki while talking about what's been going on since the last time we saw each other a couple weeks ago. She talked about work and I talked about work and my eyelash business I was starting, until Shanay shocked me with a question that had rice coming out my nose from laughter and shock.

"I'm serious, Monee. How can a bitch take the dick? When I was bigger, I couldn't take it, but I took it anyway. Now that I've lost weight, it feels like he's tearing my insides up. What should I do?"

She was serious, and I was appalled. I didn't know she was having problems in the bedroom, but since she was my best friend, I had to give her some advice.

"If it's too big, you better lube that motherfucka up. Shit, suck his shit till he cum or something. Or if it's your weight, gain your weight back. You looked good thicker anyway. Talk to your doctor too. It could be something else."

"I need you to show me how to ride dick and suck it, Monee. I know what you do for a living, even though you try to hide it. I want to set up a threesome with me, you, and my man for his b-day. I trust you enough to do this. Then you can show me how to fuck him and suck his dick."

Shanay was really giving it to me on this lunch date we were having. I had never met her husband, and I had never told Shanay anything other than me being a dancer. I kind of knew that she knew I was escorting and fucking rich niggas for money, but never brought it up.

"Girl, this is all too much. You gotta let me think about it. But threesomes are three-grand. You my bestie but I have to charge you. I've never seen your husband either. You keep him tucked like a pistol. Show me a picture so I know what I'm getting into… if I say yes."

Shanay pulled out her phone.

"He is fine as fuck, Monee, that's why I keep him tucked. We've had problems in the past, but got over them, but it's happening again. I fucking suck in the bedroom and he hates it."

She pulled up his picture, and when she showed me, my heart almost jumped out my chest. My hands were shaking as I looked at Dom's chocolate ass on her screen hugged up, smiling. I kept my cool. I never thought that he was married to my damn best friend. I couldn't say anything. She was my friend and he was my client. I had a non-disclosure with the club, I was never to speak on my clients. Eighty-five percent of them were married, so talking about them or exposing them was not an option. Not only would Shanay be pissed and probably divorce Dom, he could sue me for breaching my contract.

"You're mighty quiet, is he ugly or something?" Shanay asked. I didn't realize how quiet I had gotten.

"Nah, he isn't ugly at all. As a matter of fact, I'll do it. When is his birthday? I can use the money."

I already knew Dom's birthday. We had gotten close enough for him to tell me. I knew his name was Dominic Westbrook. I knew his birthday was November 25th and he was turning thirty-one. I also knew he was from the bay area and used to be a corner boy before he got shipped to boarding school by his grandparents. He was like my little boyfriend in my head.

"Great. I'll have the money to you this week. I'm nervous as hell but I know this whole thing will bring some fire in our bedroom."

I picked up my drink and sipped it. "Yeah, I bet it would…"

I stared off in space. I only agreed because I needed the money, and I also wanted to see Dom's face when he saw me in the room for his birthday surprise. I had been crushing on him heavy, so I wasn't missing any chance to get that dick, even if it was having a threesome with him and his wife. Shit, if Shanay was wack in bed at her age, I knew she wasn't going to ever get it. I knew Dom would be running back to me, and I still was going to be Shanay's friend. But for how long, I didn't know…

After we ate our lunch, I dropped Shanay at her house she shared with Dom. When I dropped her off, I saw Dom pulling in and stepping out his Benz I had rode in a few times. I smirked as I watched Shanay run up to Dom and shower him with hugs and kisses. He seemed interested in her. But I had a date with him in a few hours myself so I skirted off and headed home to my own mansion in the hills.

Bestie, meet my man...

Shanay

Two weeks later

I spent the whole day shopping for Dom's thirty-first birthday. I got him everything on his wish list and more. I was tired, and ready to get out the holiday traffic. It was two days after Thanksgiving and people were doing Christmas shopping. I stopped and got something to munch on while I headed home.

When I arrived home, I saw cars parked in our driveway. I had forgotten Dom had company for his birthday, so I snuck through the garage to our room to hide his gifts. I figured I'd give them to him when his guests left. I sent Monee a text letting her know I was home and we were getting the party started. I showered and dressed down in a black, tight dress with matching heels. I threw on some hoop earrings and light make-up and joined the party.

When I walked downstairs, Dom was mingling with his colleagues and a couple family members he had invited over for a party. I put on my best smile and walked over to Dom.

"Here is the leading lady here," Dom said as he kissed me on the cheek. He always made me feel wanted in front of his friends. The way he showed me off at parties, you would have thought we lived a great life and had a good sex life. Dom never treated me different in front of his friends, and it was not for show. He was truly genuine when he showed his love for me.

"No, you are the leading man tonight. It's your birthday." I took his drink from his hand and sipped it.

"Thank you, babe."

At that moment, I saw Monee walk through the door. She was dressed casual in a pencil skirt dress and slide-in gold sandals from Gucci. She had her overnight bag on her arm and her hair was long and straight. I dismissed myself from Dom and walked over to Monee. After we hugged, I walked her to my guest room and let her sit her bag down. We then headed back to the party. Dom was now standing in the kitchen talking to one of his male cousins.

"Let me take you over to meet the birthday boy," I said as I held onto Monee's hand with pride.

"I've been waiting," Monee said with a sneaky smile. She knew she wasn't there just for the party, she was there to play.

"Well, I'm not going to just lay it on him. I think we should just let the night flow so I don't scare him. By the time we get to that level, we all will be comfortable and drunk," I stated.

"I like the sound of that," Monee responded.

We walked up to Dominic and his cousin Deron. Deron didn't even let Monee get close to them good before he started drooling over her.

"Baby, I wanted you to meet a friend of mine," I said with a smile with Monee standing next to me.

"A friend? You never bring any friends around, so she must be special," Dom expressed with a smirk on his face. I could tell he was already drunk the way his hazel eyes were so glossy and slanted.

"She is special, and I want her to be our friend now. Monee, this is my husband Dominic, but you can just call him Dom. Dom, this is my best friend, Monee."

"Our friend, huh?" I watched Dom's eyes size Monee up. My friend was bad so I knew he had to take a look.

Before Dom could extended his hand, Deron stepped in. "Damn, sexy mama, it's nice to meet you. My name is Deron, I'm Dom's favorite cousin. Now how can I get to know you?" Deron boldly asked.

Monee and I started laughing. Dom put his hand on his cousin's chest gesturing for him to cool down.

"She just got here, cuz, let her get a drink or something before you start breathing down her neck," Dom spoke up.

"It's cool. He's handsome, I don't mind making a new friend. Why don't you make me something strong and I'll think about giving you my number if the drink is right." Monee winked at Deron and that had his hormones on a rise.

"You got it, lil' mama." Deron wasted no time fixing her a drink.

Me and Dom spent the night drinking and dancing around. I loved when me and Dom were on good terms. He always made me feel so special. I had never had a man make me feel like Dom made me feel, that's why I dealt with his many flaws most men had. I knew eventually he would get it together. I was hoping after he got a taste of my special birthday girl, he would definitely get his shit together because tonight, I was taking notes on everything Monee did to my man…

Birthday party

Dom

Later that night…

I nearly choked when Shanay introduced me to Monee as her best friend. All this time I had been fucking my wife's best friend and didn't know. I didn't know what they had under their sleeves, but if Monee said anything about our affair, I was going to sue her ass for breach of contract. The club I met her in was so exclusive, we had to do paperwork. No woman was to speak on the man they entertained unless they wanted to get sued. I didn't think Monee was that type of person, and my wife wasn't sneaky enough to catch me in something like this, so I kept my cool and pretended just like Monee looked like she was doing.

Monee stayed out the way most of the night, chilling and seducing my cousin Deron. That was cool with me, long as she wasn't starting trouble with my wife and trying to ruin my life. My mind still wandered though.

How did my wife know Monee?

They were the total opposite from each other. My wife worked a corporate job while Monee worked in the sex industry. I didn't want to ask Shanay anything about Monee and how they knew each other, so I went on with my night like she wasn't even there.

It was getting late and people were still partying at my house. Everyone was drunk, still eating up my birthday cake and drinking all the free liquor. I saw Shanay sitting on the couch, opening a fresh bottle of Moet with Monee.

"Oh, they trying to get super drunk," I said to myself. It didn't look like Monee was going anywhere anytime soon. She looked over intoxicated, and I couldn't lie, she was looking good as hell. I kind of wanted a taste of her for my birthday, but I knew Shanay was going to be trying to throw her wack ass sex on me as a birthday gift to end the night.

Shanay spotted me near the kitchen and walked over to me.

"Let's go to the room for a second, I need to talk to you," she said while grabbing my hand.

We walked up to our room and I flopped on the bed. It felt so good to lay on my memory foam bed, I didn't want to get up. Shanay lifted me up to sit up on the bed.

"You fucked up, huh?" Shanay asked with a slight laugh.

"Hell yeah, I'm ready to get in this bed," I admitted.

"Well not just yet. I got so many gifts for you, it's going to take a couple days to recover from them. But let's have a serious conversation since we only have these talks when we are drunk. Tell the truth, why do you keep stepping out on me and not wanting to work out our problems? Do I disgust you?" she asked in a sympathetic tone. She had caught me off guard but I knew I couldn't brush her off.

"You don't disgust me, Nay, you are my dream girl. You are just different now. Ever since you lost weight, things have changed in the bedroom. You suck babe, and I need pussy," I boldly said.

She sighed. "I knew I shouldn't have lost all this weight. I thought I would feel better and make you stick around. I know I'm not that good in the bed room either, but I'm willing to learn to please you."

"Babe, I'm sorry if I'm putting so much pressure on you, but sex is a big part of our relationship. You used to take the dick good, now it's like I'm fucking a virgin every time and it's so frustrating. When you try to go down on me, you act like you've never done it before. I just need you to snap out your funk and get your groove back." Hell, she told me to be truthful so I was.

"Well, after tonight, all of that will change. I've decided to gain at least ten pounds back and get better in the bedroom. But I want to show you your gifts I got you." Shanay rushed over to the closet and started pulling bags from the closet.

 As she got my gifts out, I thought about what she had said. I was pleased that she was going to gain some weight and I was pleased she was willing to get it together in the bedroom. I was hoping her getting it together would stop me from seeing Monee. Because after finding out she was my wife's best friend and Shanay was willing to change, I figured it was time to end it.

Shanay came out the closet with so much stuff for me. This woman had gotten everything I had been talking about for the last few months. New Rolex, new diamond earrings, new Gucci jacket, and she even got me new Versace draws and socks.

"I figured you needed those," she said with a smile. She knew how I loved a fresh pair of expensive underwear.

"Thank you, babe. Let's go get rid of our company so we can enjoy the night."

When we said our goodbyes to everyone, I noticed Monee stayed. She helped Shanay clean up and they talked a little. I was ready for her ass to leave so I could go to sleep or see what else my wife had in store for me. I sat on the couch and listened to the soft R&B sounds Alexa was playing. I closed my eyes and kicked off my loafers. A few minutes into closing my eyes I felt my wife massaging my arms. She then slid her hand down my unbuttoned shirt. I smirked and opened my eyes. When I looked up, it was not Shanay, it was Monee. I jumped up. I knew she had to be out her mind trying to seduce me while my wife was home. That's when I heard my wife laugh. She stepped in front of me in a small white bra and matching lace thong.

"It's okay, baby. I told her to get close to you. This is the second part of your present."

Monee and Shanay stood in front of me looking like two snacks. I thought I was dreaming, but clearly I wasn't. Monee fell to her knees and started undoing my belt while my wife tongue kissed me with a bottle of champagne in her hand and a blunt.

"You are the king tonight baby. Let us please you," my wife said in a sexy tone. She was in rare form and I liked it. She handed me the lit blunt and champagne bottle.

I was so absolutely turned on by these two that I had forgotten that I had even fucked Monee before. Tonight, she was different. It was as though she was a teacher for Shanay to please me. Shanay watched her suck on my dick like a pro while she stood back and sipped her wine.

"Now you come do it just like I did," I heard Monee say, and Shanay did just that.

Shanay took my dick to the back of her throat and gagged. She started sliding my dick in and out her mouth while she gripped on my balls like Monee was doing, and had always done. She was driving me wild. I grabbed a hand full of her hair and she really got into it.

Monee walked over to the coffee table and picked up a bottle of lubricant and a condom. She slid the condom on me and slid down my pole. She moaned loudly as my ten inches touched her guts. As she rode me slow, Monee and Shanay began to kiss. My dick was rock hard then so I started thrusting from under her. After riding me for five minutes, she got off me and started rubbing lube on my dick and Shanay's pussy.

"Now get on top and ride him like I did," Monee said.

Shanay slowly slid down my dick as Monee helped her. My wife was so tight but she was taking it like a pro. She rode me slow until she got used to my dick. She started to speed up as I sucked on Monee's titties and played with her pussy with my fingers. I couldn't believe I was having a threesome with my wife and a stripper I was fucking behind her back, that happened to be her best friend.

Wild shit, huh?

When we got to the bedroom things got freakier. Monee and Shanay were taking turns with my dick, and I was loving it. Monee was coaching Shanay through the whole thing and I liked it. Shanay was taking every inch of me while Monee rooted her on.

"That's right, bitch, ride that shit. It feel good, don't it?" Monee smacked Shanay on the ass causing her to moan louder.

Monee bent over on the bed and so did Shanay. I dipped in and out of both of them. I felt like I was in a porno and I couldn't believe Shanay was into all this nasty shit. We kept going at it while drinking and smoking while music played throughout the house. This was definitely my best birthday ever, and I wasn't going to forget it.

After our three-hour threesome, I was worn out. Monee had already tapped out and went to our guestroom while me and Shanay continued, but I was beat. However, I needed to talk to Shanay. She was a different person in the threesome and I was hoping that Shanay was staying.

"Babe, before you close your eyes, let me ask you a question… what made you want to have a threesome?"

She chuckled a little. "To bring some spice into this bedroom, and to teach me how to fuck you. Monee taught me some things. And I know once I get my ass thick again, I'll really be throwing it back on you. I love you and I really want us to be together forever, start our family, and ball out on our success. We are made for each other and I understand why you stepped out. But I'm going to make sure it doesn't happen again. So once I master all your needs like you did mine, and you still cheat on me, it's over for good. So cherish me wanting to change for you because I didn't have to," she stated boldly, and I took it all in.

"Well I appreciate everything you have done for our relationship. I loved everything about tonight and I hope this Shanay is staying around."

"Yup, this Shanay is here to stay long as you stay true to me here on out."

"You definitely don't have to worry about me stepping out. I love you."

"I love you too."

After my birthday, I was everything Shanay wanted and she was the same. Our sex life was amazing now, and we were back on track as a couple. I was coming home on time every night and Shanay was even cooking again. I thought everything would be cool between me and Monee, but boy was I wrong…

Come see Me

Monee

One Week Later…

I sat looking in my phone while my mother talked my ear off about how she hated the nursing home she lived in. I loved my mother and I knew she took care of me all my life, but I didn't have time to take care of her on my own at home. She had too many demands so keeping her in a nursing home while I worked was good for me. I paid a hundred-grand every six months for her to stay here. She lived like a queen in this place but still had something to complain about all the time.

"That lady gave me my insulin with the wrong needle, Monee. I told you they need more schooling, they don't know nothin'!" my mother shouted, causing me to look up from my phone. I wasn't interested in her complaints, I was too busy trying to contact Dom. It had been a week since the threesome and I hadn't heard from his ass. I knew he was all up under Shanay enjoying what I had taught her, and I felt some kind of way about that shit and he needed to know it.

"Ma, people make mistakes. You got your meds, right?"

"Yeah, as much money as we give them, you would think she would remember to use a small needle. And who the hell you over there dialing? You know I hate those damn cell phones. I caught ya daddy cheating with a cell phone. You need to stay off them social medias and Bookface and find you something else to do like knit me a sweater."

I blurted out laughing. "Knit you a sweater?"

"Yes, instead of letting men control your life. You think ion know what you be out here doing? I'm your mother. You gotta do something with yaself,

Monee. Don't be like your brother. I ain't raise you like that."

I heard my mother and as much as it stung, she was right. But men were my money maker so what she was asking wasn't happening no time soon. I let her continue as I texted Dom a fucked up text.

ME: If you don't meet me tonight, I'm telling Shanay. You think I give a fuck about a best friend? I got money to pay a lawsuit!

Dom wasted no time texting me back after I left that text.

DOM DADDY: Shoot me your address so we can talk in private…

I smirked, feeling like I had gotten my way like I always did with men. Dom knew he couldn't leave this pussy alone. It was golden and way better than Shanay's. I had to teach the bitch everything, now Dom wanted to act like I wasn't the one that made his marriage better.

"Ma, I gotta go. I'll make sure they give you the right needle next time. I'll be back some time tomorrow." I kissed her on the forehead and headed out to my whip.

When I got home, I fed my Yorkie and then took a long bath. I was going to be looking sexy when Dominic came to my door. So good, his ass wasn't going to want to leave me…

It's over

Dom

7 pm

Monee had been blowing me the fuck up. At first, I was brushing her off, then she got too serious for me.

Mo: If you don't meet with me, I'll break this contract and tell your wife! You think I give a fuck about a best friend, nigga!? I got money to pay a lawsuit!" was the last text I read from her.

Me: Send me your address, we need to talk in private…

I texted her back and headed out my office. I was done with her ass and I wasn't looking back. After the threesome, Shanay did a full flip on me. The threesome had turned her into a beast, and I no longer needed Monee's attention. I was hoping she understood that since she already knew why she was invited into my bedroom, but she had things twisted. She had caught feelings for me which I already knew was coming ever since she came on my dick for the first time. I had taken things too far with Monee, now I had to figure a way out of it without hurting my wife.

I pulled up to her mansion in the hills and parked on the street. I marched up to her door. Before I could start banging on her door, it flew open. She stood in the doorway wearing a white silk robe, showing off cleavage and much thigh.

Damn, why did this vindictive bitch have to open the door looking so good? I said to myself, but I kept myself in control. It was over between me and Monee. I was ready to commit to my wife.

"What's up, Dominic? I knew I could get your sexy ass over here some way, somehow. I know you not about to let that threesome and the fact that your wife is my best friend get in the way of us," she said in a sassy tone.

She stood to the side and let me walk in her foyer.

"There was nothing between us, Monee. I paid you for your services, now you catching feelings? You need to go ahead on with your life," I expressed.

Monee walked up to me and wrapped her arms around my waist. She looked up at me and smiled.

"Come on, Dom. You know you gonna miss this pussy. Just hit it one more time for free. I promise I won't tell Shanay."

"I didn't come over here to fuck and make a deal, Monee. I can't fuck you no more, free or not. I never had feelings for you in the first place so don't play yourself in this situation. Let it go." I took her hands from around my waist.

Monee stunned me with a slap across my face. The fire in her eyes let me know she was offended, but I didn't give a fuck.

"You need to chill, Monee, with putting your hands on me. Don't think I won't fuck you up because you a female. If you know a nigga, you know I ain't no bitch. So keep your fucking hands off me." I gave her a look that could kill, but she didn't care. At this moment, this was when I knew Monee's ass was crazy.

"You ARE a bitch, Dom! You think you hard, nigga! I'll tell Shanay right now and ruin your life and let the real bitch in you come out!"

Monee charged at me with her fist swinging like a wild woman. I felt her sharp cat nails dig through my left cheek. I snapped. I grabbed her by the throat and pinned her to the couch. She grabbed me by my button-down dress shirt and ripped it open. I was breathing heavy and I was pissed the fuck off. I hadn't been so mad in so long, I really didn't know how to control myself. I pressed down harder, trying to stop her from breathing. She had me fucked up and I was ready to kill her ass. I had dealt with crazy women in the past and knew you had to play the crazy role with them to calm them down.

"Bitch, you think I give a fuck about your life, you tacky ass hoe, bitch. You tell Shanay anything, I swear I'll kill you, bitch. I got a shotgun that will blow your fucking face off and enough money to make you disappear. Now I said this shit is over, so if I hear anything about you saying anything, I'll fucking kill you, bitch. You hear me, bitch? Say yeah," I gritted at her in a demanding tone. I could see the fear in her eyes and I loved it. I had her right where I wanted her. Scared…

She shook her head yes as much as she could. I let her throat go and stood up. She held her neck and caught her breath.

"Get the fuck out!" she shouted, pointing to the door.

"Gladly," I said in a calm tone. I heard her screaming and crying as I left but didn't feel sorry for her. I was done, and moving on with my life.

When I got inside my car, I felt my cheek stinging. I pulled down my visor and looked in the mirror. My face was bleeding. Monee had left three scratches on my face. They weren't that deep, but they were visible on my black ass. I knew I couldn't go home with my face and clothes looking like this. Plus I was in a bad space and I couldn't face Shanay at the moment. I had to get away for a couple days. I decided to drive to Vegas and stay for a couple days to get my mind right and then back to work before heading home. Hopefully my scratches wouldn't be so noticeable by the time I went back home.

I sighed and picked up my cellphone. I had to call Shanay and tell her I wouldn't be home. When she answered I told her I was going to Arizona for an impromptu business meeting. Shanay understood and told me to be safe.

After I hung up with her, I stopped at the weed dispensary and the gas station and loaded up on gas and snacks. I then headed to the highway and did 80 on the empty road all the way to Las Vegas.

When I got to Vegas, I booked me a room at the MGM casino and hotel. I bought a bottle of Hennessy and played craps until I ran out of pocket change. I didn't win a dime and the liquor didn't make me feel any better. I walked the strip and smoked blunt after blunt in the cool midnight air. All I could think about was all the wrong I caused Shanay. I was truly a fucked up husband to her and if anything bad was to happen to me, I knew it would be from karma. As much as I made her unhappy, she did everything she could to please me. Any man in their right mind would appreciate that alone, but I was always selfish. Now I was ready to change, but I was in a deep hole. I had to figure things out fast before shit got out of control.

After walking two miles on the strip, I headed back to my room. So many beautiful women were trying to get my attention, but I was bitter and already in enough shit with women. I went to my room and passed out.

I woke up the next morning groggy and irritated. I rolled a blunt to calm my nerves and sat on the balcony. I felt at ease but when I looked at my phone, I had so many missed calls. I called my office and told them to cancel all my meetings for the next couple days. I decided to turn off my phone and work from my laptop. I had some decisions to make so I spent the day trying to figure if I wanted to come clean to Shanay.

By the time I checked out later that night, I still had no clue what I wanted to do. This bitch Monee had me stuck, and it wasn't anybody else's fault but my own...

$$$$

Three days later…

I sat in my office in deep thought as my co-worker and best friend Richard sat in front of me calling off food places on Door Dash. It was lunch time and I was starving, but I couldn't get my mind off this situation with Monee and Shanay. I hadn't been home in three days because I was hiding from Shanay until the scratches on my face healed. I was still baffled that they were best friends. I didn't know they were friends. Had I known, I wouldn't have fucked around with her. I had told her all my problems. She knew about my infidelities and everything I felt about Shanay when we were having problems. I didn't want Shanay to know any of the negative things I had said about her in the past to another woman. I knew she would be embarrassed and would fall back into her slump she was in.

"Yo, man, I said do you want Chinese or pizza?" Richard asked loudly, snapping me out my thoughts.

"My bad, bro. Let's do pizza. I got a lot of work to do and Chinese makes a nigga sleepy," I responded as I looked at the time on my Frank Muller. I had a lot of work to do and had to be done by three, but I couldn't focus. Too much was going on in my personal life. I had to go home with scratches on my face. I knew Shanay was going to be suspicious.

"What's going on man? You aight?" he asked.

"Yeah, I'm good."

"Yeah right, I know that gaze. Having trouble in paradise?" he asked with a smirk as he rubbed his cheek, referring to the scratches on my face.

"A lil', but nothing I can't handle."

"Well whatever it is, don't let it end in divorce. You see what happened to me. I make a three hundred-grand salary a year and I'm living in a pizza box apartment. It's cheaper to keep her, bro."

Confession

Shanay

I stood in the kitchen making me and Dominic some dinner. He was due to be home any moment so I wanted everything prepared upon his arrival. I had missed him so much over the last two days. He had to go on an unexpected business trip, so I knew he would be looking for some sex and a home cooked meal. Things had been going great for us, and I wanted to keep it that way so I was tending to his needs as much as I could.

As I sat and waited, I sent Monee a text. I had been texting her since she left my house the day after the party, but she wasn't responding. I was hoping the whole ordeal didn't make her feel weird or feel like we couldn't be close anymore, because I really valued our friendship. I had known Monee since I was in high school. She always had my back and I had hers. I knew I could trust her with my life, that's why I trusted her with my man. But the way she wasn't getting back to me had me kind of regretting getting her to coach me.

I was snapped out my thoughts when I heard my front door slam and security alarm beep through the house. I knew it was Dom, so I stood up from the dinner table and walked back over to the stove to check on my greens.

"Damn, babe, you got it smelling good up in here. Is that country greens I smell?" Dom wrapped his arms around my waist and kissed me on the neck.

"You know it. I baked some chicken and made some mac and cheese too. I figured you would like a home cooked meal."

"You already know I do. Let me go take a shower and get comfortable. I'm off for the next few days, let's just stay home and relax."

"I'm down, I have three days off myself."

Dom walked out the kitchen and headed upstairs to shower. I opened a bottle of wine and pulled out the glasses. I sat two plates on the table and started piling it with food, especially mine. I was on a mission to get my body back so carbs and crunches were my best friends now.

Dom came downstairs in a pair of black Gucci boxer briefs I had gotten him for his birthday. His ripped chest was looking smooth and sexy, and I could tell he had been in the gym lately. I bit down on my bottom lip, lusting over my husband.

"You would come down here looking like a snack after being gone two days. How was your trip anyway?" I asked as we sat at the table.

"It was okay. Same as the others," he said nonchalantly.

"Okay. Well let's eat…"

As we ate, I noticed Dom was unusually quiet. He focused on his food and drank glass after glass of wine. He didn't seem like himself, so I studied his face and body language before I asked him what was wrong. His body was a little tense, but the scars I spotted on his face were out of the ordinary and had red flags flying in my face.

"Dom, what happened to your cheek?" I asked, causing him to drop his fork.

He looked down at his food and then he looked up at me. I was already disappointed. I knew it was something that had to do with a woman. It was clear the scars came from fingernails. I was already pissed, but I let him dig his grave.

"I was waiting for you to ask me, and I'm ready to tell you the truth." He paused, trying to peep my demeanor. And I'm sure it showed, I was definitely upset and all ears. I crossed my legs and my arms while cocking my head to the side. I raised my eyebrow, giving him much attitude. "I'm fucking listening…"

"I haven't been honest with you at all, and if you want to divorce me after this confession you could. I've been sleeping with Monee, but I never knew she was your best friend…"

I stood up from my seat. "You've been doing what?!" I shouted. I was full of rage and feeling betrayed.

"Is that why the bitch won't answer my calls because she is your little side bitch?! How long have you been sleeping with that nasty bitch, Dom?! I'm going to have to get tested for AIDS." I walked up to him and pushed him so hard he almost fell out his chair. The look in his eyes showed he knew he had me fucked up.

"Shanay, listen. I didn't know she was your friend. The only reason why I have these scratches is because I went to call things off with her and she got mad and scratched me. But I'm done with her, I promise."

"Oh, you bet you are done with that bitch, and I'm done with your ass too! Pack your shit and get the fuck out my house! Go live with that hoe ass bitch! Did you know she lives in the strip club, sucking dick!? That bitch don't own that mansion she lives in! She lives in Air B&B houses, you dummy! That bitch ain't shit but a gold digging, man stealing, rat bitch. And when I catch her, I'm going to beat her ass!" I shouted. I picked up the wine bottle and tossed it across the room. Red wine and glass shattered all over my white carpet, making me madder.

"Get the fuck out, Dominic!" I shouted and headed to my garage. I jumped in his Lamborghini truck and drove off. Fuck him! I was going to drive this motherfucker till the wheels were flat. He didn't give a damn about me, so I didn't give a damn about him…

ROBIN

$$$$$

Two days later…

I turned off my phone for two days. Luckily I didn't have to work, because my ass would have been fired for a no call, no show. After riding out in Dominic's truck till the gas ran out, I came home and he was gone. He didn't call me when I left asking about his car because he knew had he said the wrong thing to me, I would have totaled his two hundred-grand whip.

I spent two days crying and asking myself what the fuck was wrong with me, and I came up with nothing. I was good looking, smart, and treated my man well. But yet he went out and slept with Monee. My damn best friend, somebody I thought I could trust. I figured they didn't know they had ties to me before the threesome because I had never showed Dom to Monee and vice versa. But I knew Monee knew she had been messing with Dom when I showed her his picture, yet she still didn't say anything. She went on with the threesome, took my money, and now she was dodging me. I hadn't called her yet. I needed to clear my mind first. I knew I was going to beat her ass either way, but I wanted a clear head when I did it.

I looked at the time on my clock and it was seven in the evening on a Saturday. I decided to turn on my phone and see what was going on in the world. Soon as my phone powered up, I had numerous texts from Dom. I decided to read them to see him begging.

DOM: Nay, please call me. I'm sorry and I miss you. Can you call and at least let me know you are okay?

DOM: I really want to work things out with you, babe. I'm staying at my mother's so you can have your space. I'm not with Monee or any other woman. I'm here at my mom's. She knows everything. I told her, and she is of course siding with you. Can you at least call or meet with her?

I loved Dom's mother, but I wasn't ready to talk to anyone about my situation so I ignored his text and made it a mental note to call his mom after the weekend.

I then checked my Facebook and saw that my little sister had in-boxed me the night before. I had forgotten I had a little sister with all the bullshit in my life, and it was her birthday. I looked at her message and she sent me a club flyer. I hadn't been to a club in so long, but decided to take her up on her invite. I needed to get out and move around, and possibly get drunk. My little sister was only twenty-five, and I was twenty-seven. She was a wild girl, so I knew I would get a little loose. I decided to give her a call to let her know I was coming.

"Sister! Where have you been? You been locked in with that rich nigga Dom, and forgot you had a family," my sister said before I could say hello.

"Happy b-day, baby sis. I've been working. You know I'm just as rich as my husband. But what's up with this party? I'm coming."

"Hell yeah, my sister gonna be in the house. It's in Hollywood. I already got the VIP section on lock for us so just pull up and valet. I'll put your name on my list."

"Cool… How about I pick you up. I just purchased a Lambo truck. Let's floss like we used to," I said with a smile. I still had Dom's truck, so I was going to continue to floss in it. We were married so what was his was mine, and he wasn't getting this truck back.

"I'm down with that! I'll be ready in two hours. I love you, sis, and thank you."

I made me a quick meal and then headed to the shower. After I showered, I headed to my closet and found something to wear. I decided on a little red silk Valentino dress with matching stilettoes. I unwrapped my hair and then put on some gold and diamonds. After filling my Chanel handbag with everything I needed, I headed out the door. I decided to book me a room because I had plans on not coming home tonight. Even if I left the club alone, I was booking me a penthouse suite for the next two days and continue to get my mind right without anything of Dominic's around. My house was too depressing and I couldn't take it any longer.

Ex best friend

Monee

That same night…

I sat in my stylist's chair watching her glue my fresh pink lace front to my head. I was loving my new, soft, pink wig and I couldn't wait to show it off on Instagram. It had been a couple days since me and Dominic had our fight and I was finally feeling like myself again. I had shut down like this nigga had broken up with me and we had been together for years. But I was back to being Monee and I had money to make. So I was getting my hair done and stepping out with this rich rapper named Lee. He was the hottest rapper in Atlanta and he wanted me to be his LA girl. Of course I charged his ass up and he paid me ten grand to be his for the weekend. I was so glad he asked me because I probably would still be contemplating on telling Shanay and starting drama with them. I figured I would let it go, and even thought about calling Shanay to do lunch. Dom's soft ass was replaceable, and I knew I could find better.

"Girl, this wig is bomb. You know everybody is going to want this same wig," my stylist said as she started brushing through my wig. It was so straight and soft, I was contemplating to make this my good wig.

"I know, but shit, more money for you. You know I don't care about no female taking my style," I said as I handed her the four hundred-dollar bills I was holding.

After brushing through it once more, I was out the door and headed home. I looked at the time and it was eight in the evening. I got in my car and headed home. As I headed home, my phone began to ring. It was my Atlanta boo Lee. I smiled and picked up my phone.

"What's up, baby, you ready for me?" I asked when I picked up the phone.

"You know I am, baby girl. I'll be in front your door in an hour, so be that ass ready," he said through the phone with his thick country accent. It was so sexy to me.

"I sure will, daddy."

I rushed home and got dressed. I already knew what I was wearing so after I showered, I slid in a red Valentino dress I had gotten a while back after seeing Shanay in the same dress. I slid on a pair of red heels and added my accessories. I brushed my pink ass hair and then headed to my kitchen for a drink. After three shots of Hennessy, Lee was texting me to come outside. When I stepped outside my house, it looked like a luxury car show. Lee pulled up in a black Maserati truck, with Bentleys, Mercedes, and Porches following behind him.

"Damn, this nigga came out here to stunt. He better hope he don't get robbed," I joked to myself as I walked up to his truck.

When I got in, the car had a cloud of smoke floating around with a backseat full of gold mouth, dreadhead niggas. I really wasn't feeling him having a car full of niggas our first time meeting. But I kept my cool and put on a smile.

"Damn, this bitch bad right here, boy, you gonna have to pass her," one of the men said in the back seat.

"Fall back, bruh. She's mine for the weekend. You gotta book her on ya own time," he said, letting everyone know I was a hoe.

"Damn, nigga, just put me on blast before you even say hello," I shot at Lee. His boys laughed.

"Girl, you better calm down. I'm paying for this so I can say whatever I want."

"Whatever, since it's like that then, let's get this shit over with. I'm ready to hit the club."

When we got to the club, it was jumping but I was so bored. Lee had me sitting in his section watching him conduct business and drink lean. He was being controlling and didn't want anyone to talk to me. I was so annoyed, and I had a fat blunt in my purse so I snuck out the section and headed to the patio smoking section.

When I got outside, the cool breeze took away some of my irritation. I reached into my clutch bag for my lighter and blunt. As I stood over the balcony, listening to the slow Jamaican music the outside DJ was playing while smoking my blunt, I looked out at Hollywood Blvd. I remembered when I was a prostitute walking down Hollywood with my friends. The money was good, but the men were disgusting. I was eighteen when I walked the streets until I was recruited into the private club I worked for. I vowed I would never be a street walker again.

As I blew smoke out my nose, I felt someone tap my shoulder. When I turned around, it was Shanay. She stood wearing the same dress as me, but she was wearing a mean mug on her face.

"Damn, you want my man and my style too, huh, bitch?" Shanay said in a drunken slur.

"For real, Shanay?" I asked with an attitude. I figured Dom's bitch ass had told on himself to save his marriage. But I kept my cool with her.

"Yes for real, bitch. I let you in my bed with my man, and you already been sleeping with him. Why didn't you tell me, Monee? I thought you were my friend."

"You better watch who you call a friend then, because I don't consider nobody a friend of mine. We were close, and as far as Dom, I didn't know he was your man until we had that threesome. So don't come at me like I knew he was your man. I was paid for my services, but I have to admit, we had a connection. I mean, you weren't fucking him right, the man had to do something." I smirked. Since she confronted me, I wanted to get under her skin.

"Monee, you ain't shit but a trash ass bitch. When I showed you Dom's picture you could have told me the deal then, but you took my money and fucked my man right in my face. You and Dom ain't shit. Y'all are made for each other. So take his raggedy ass in and keep 'em!"

Shanay took her drink and tossed it on me. I looked down and saw that my dress was ruined. I grabbed Shanay by her hair and all hell broke loose. Once I let Shanay's hair go, I slipped on a wet area and that's when Shanay got the best of me. The bitch punched me in my mouth and my face. When I tried to get a hold of her, she grabbed me by my lace front and ripped it from my edges. I felt a strong man grab me and toss me to the side. I looked over the men and saw security carrying Shanay out the patio area. It was Lee that was holding me back, and he didn't look happy. I had probably fucked my money up, but it wasn't my fault. I looked on the ground and saw my wig. I was too embarrassed to pick it up. *Four hundred down the drain.*

"Fuck you, Monee. We will never be friends again. You fucking whore!" was the last thing I heard her say before they drug her out.

This bitch had pulled my wig off in front of the whole club, embarrassing me. Shanay was going to pay, and so was Dominic because this shit was all his fault.

Mother-in-law

Shanay

I drove to my hotel suite mad as hell. I had left my sister at the club, and her and Dom were blowing up my phone. Monee must have called his ass and told him we had a fight, but I didn't give a fuck. Accidently answering my phone, Dom spoke quickly through the Bluetooth system in his truck I was riding around in.

"Baby, what the fuck happened?" he asked.

"I had a fight with your side bitch, Monee, that's what the fuck happened! You thought I was playing when I said I was going to catch her and beat her ass?!" I shouted through the speakers.

"Well, it's all over fucking social media that y'all had a fight over me. Are you fucking crazy? Do you know how detrimental that is to both our fucking jobs?" he gritted.

"That's all you fucking care about Dominic, is your image! You wasn't thinking about your image when you was fucking that nasty bitch. Now is not the time. If you ain't calling to fix it, get the fuck off my line."

"Nay, I'm sorry. I never meant for all of this to go this far. Why the hell were you in the club anyway?"

"Because! You pushed me to step out and see if I still had it. I'm going to find me a new nigga, Dominic Rijon Thomas, that appreciates me and will love me for all my flaws."

At that moment, his mother, Ann, grabbed his phone.

"Shanay, baby girl, I'm so sorry you are going through all this. I love you like a daughter and I really want to talk to you. Please come by so we can all sit down and talk about this foolishness," his mother pleaded, putting me in a bad space. I couldn't say no, but I couldn't completely say yes.

I sighed… "Mrs. Thomas, I really didn't want to drag you into this. Dominic is a dog and I don't think this is going to last. But give me a couple days. I'll be by after work on Monday." I dismissed the call.

I drove back to the club and picked up my sister and her friends. She so happened to have a suite at the same hotel as me, so we all headed back to her suite. I sat up all night drinking and talking with my sister and her old friends.

"Bitch, I told you that bitch Monee wasn't shit since we were all in school. She is envious, and I wouldn't put it past her if she knew Dom was your man all along. Men always say women are naive, but they are just as much as we are. Dom fell in her trap and couldn't get out. But are you going to forgive him?" my sister asked.

"I don't know what I'm going to do. It isn't like we are boyfriend and girlfriend anymore, so I can't just walk away. I'll keep you updated tho'." I sipped my margarita.

"Yea, next time I see that bitch Monee I'ma beat her ass too. I wish I was right there, I would have jumped in."

We all laughed. I smoked and drank with my sister till the sun came up. After we ate breakfast, I went to my penthouse suite, took a shower, and fell into a deep sleep when I got out. I was so exhausted, I didn't wake up for fifteen hours…

$$$$

Two days later…

I was fresh off work, and I had just remembered I told Dom's mom I would be over after work for dinner. I was still a little irritated with the whole situation, but she called me and told me she was cooking, and Dom's mom was a beast in the kitchen, so I was headed straight there. Still driving Dom's truck, I started it up. It sounded a little weird when it started up. I had been driving his car all around, hardly putting gas and never checked to see if it needed oil. Hell, this was an expensive car, it shouldn't be breaking down anyway.

I drove out my parking lot at work and headed to the east side of LA. Dom's mom wanted to stay right in the hood. She had a nice home, but she loved that environment for some reason. I guess it reminded her of The Bay. I didn't mind because I was a hood chick too.

I pulled up and saw Dom's Mercedes and his mom's Cadillac truck parked in the driveway. I parked on the street and stepped out. It was three in the afternoon on a Monday, so everyone was on the block, and all eyes were on me and Dom's truck. I smiled, waved, and kept it pushing to Mrs. Thomas' door. I rang the bell and the door opened right up.

"Shanay, I'm so glad you decided to come. Sit down, take off your heels. I know you been in that office all day," Mrs. Thomas stated as she walked me into the living room.

"I definitely need to take my heels off. I was on my feet all day, conducting meetings."

"You know you are the star of that company. They love you." She smiled and sat next to me.

"Yeah, I know. And I love what I do. So what's going on? Where's Dom?" I asked.

"He's in the shower. The boy has been locked in his father's home gym blasting music and working out. I told him he was going to look like the Hulk by the time he worked out all his frustrations." She chuckled, and I did the same. That's what Dom did when he was horny and couldn't get none. He would work out until his muscles couldn't take it no more.

"Oh, okay. Well I guess we can talk alone while he's upstairs."

"Ya, let's go out to my garden for some fresh air."

Me and Mrs. Thomas walked outside to her gardens. I loved going out to her garden. It was a little windy because it was fall season and the Santa Ana winds made their way to the hood, but the sun that was hidden behind her apple tree was keeping us warm. Mrs. Thomas grew lavender, aloe vera, apples, and roses. So her garden smelled amazing and always put me at ease. We sat on her wooden bench swing and gazed at her lavender bushes flow through the wind. I closed my eyes and listened to the wind blow in the trees. For the first time in almost a month, I felt good.

"I remember the reason why I did my backyard this way. I was going through a divorce with Dominic's father, and I needed something to keep my anxiety down, so I planted a garden. The lavender was the one thing that saved me. It kept me out of a mental institution and off drugs," Mrs. Thomas stated calmly. I didn't say anything, I just continued to listen.

"After my divorce, five years later, I let his father back in. He was diagnosed with cancer, and I couldn't just let him die alone. We rekindled our love and he got better. He was only thirty-five years old when he was diagnosed with cancer, and he was back on his feet in a year. He was strong enough to cheat again, but we learned a lot about each other through his sickness. He learned to love me for me and I did the same. Sometimes it takes a man to hit rock bottom before he changes his life for the one he truly loves. But it's all on you if you want to stick by him or not."

"Well I hope this situation is his rock bottom for him because I'm ready to let it all go." I crossed my arms. I could feel my attitude flaring.

"What the hell happened? You were just here a couple weeks ago for Thanksgiving, you two were happy. Now everything hit the fan."

"He's been sleeping with my best friend, and they claim they both didn't know I was in the picture. I found out a couple nights after his birthday after a night of partying together. I'm just sick of all the cheating and the lies. I've done so much to change for him and he just isn't satisfied." I could feel myself tearing up, but I held them back.

"Don't let no man make you change who you are. One thing I didn't do was change for my husband. I left him because if he wasn't happy with me, I can do bad by myself. Forget what's on ya heart because the heart will have you in a bad space, what's on ya mind?" she asked.

"My heart is broken, it's my mind that wants me to make this work. I spoke with my therapist in a text message and she told me to seek marriage counseling."

Mrs. Thomas nodded her head. "Do what's best for you, baby. Whatever happens with you and my son, just know I'm still here for you. I'll never love another female like a daughter like I've done you. You are a good woman, don't let my son strip you away from your sanity," she admitted. I really appreciated Dom's mother. She had been through a lot and always held her head up high. One thing she never did was show a weak side, and I really admired that.

"Thanks for the talk, but I think someone is ready to talk too," I said when I noticed Dom standing in the back door watching me and his mother. He had a blunt rolled in his ear and a glass of dark liquor in a glass. His mother stood up.

"I'll be inside getting dinner on the table," she said and walked off.

Dominic held the door open for his mother and let her walk in. After he made sure she safely made it inside, he walked over to me. I watched Dom walk over to me. He was so damn handsome, but yet so rugged. If he didn't always wear business casual clothes or suits on the regular, you would have thought he was a thug. That was one reason I was so infatuated with this man. His demeanor was everything. But I wasn't going to let it get the best of me this time. I was so close to letting our relationship go.

"What's up, wifey? How are you feeling today?" Dom asked as he fired up his blunt.

"I'm a little better today. How have you been?"

No matter how mad me and Dom were at each other, we always made sure we were okay mentally. It was just something we did, and that was one of the many reasons I loved this man.

"I'm not okay. I want to come home and work things out."

I picked up his drink that was sitting by his foot and sipped it.

"How long were y'all sleeping together behind my back? Because I don't believe that you two didn't know we all had ties."

"Shanay, when have you ever introduced me to anybody other than your sister, and the women in your family? I would never have slept with her if I had known, I swear."

"Dom, why would you cheat on me in the first place? I know we were having problems in the bedroom, but you knew we were working to fix that. Why keep hurting me? You see what it cost us. It cost me a friend and our marriage. I just want to know why?"

"I met her at a strip party. Deron's bachelor party to be exact. I don't know, I just kept going back to her for pleasure. I didn't know she had caught feelings for me until the night I left you at our dinner table, but I have no feelings for her, never did. I didn't know she was your best friend until the threesome. We had never talked about her friends or family. I swear, I did not know," he pleaded and then hit his blunt so hard, he started coughing from the smoke he inhaled.

I sighed and finished off his drink. I was so torn. I loved Dominic, and Monee was my best friend. At least I thought she was. The way she spoke to me before we fought let me know she probably would have still slept with Dominic if she knew he was my husband. She didn't consider me as a friend, all she cared about was sex and money. After hearing that, I figured I'd let our friendship die and try to see if I could make things right with Dominic. I knew men came a dime a dozen, but I wasn't repairing anything with a bitch that didn't consider me as a friend anyway.

"You have ninety days to get your shit together and prove to me that you are here for me and only me. I'm not going to tolerate any more of your childish bullshit. We're going to counseling to see what the hell is wrong with you. Once we finish ten sessions,

I'll think about if I want to stay married to you," I laid the law down. We had been together five years and only the last two years have been bad. I was willing to repair our marriage only if he was willing to put in the work.

He passed his blunt to me as he answered to my ultimatum.

"I'll go to counseling, hell I'll cut my dick off if I have to, long as I can be with you. Now can I please come home? I know it's too soon, but you know how my mama is. She had me clean her house top to bottom. Literally, I cleaned her ceiling and all her walls. She don't care if a nigga gotta work, she have me and Pops up at midnight scrubbing floors. That military in her ain't no joke."

I blurted out laughing. "That's funny, but I'm still mad. You can't sleep in my bed, but you can sleep in the guesthouse. When you get a clean bill of health from STDS and HIV, you can come back in the house, but in the guest room."

"Damn, I guess that's cool, but I'm clean. I'll go get checked again for you, tho'. I love you, Shanay, and I'm sorry for all my bullshit. I feel like this whole situation is my fault and my wakeup call. I won't ever fuck around again."

"Yeah, I hear you. You can come home in a couple days. I'll have the cleanup guys come clean out the guesthouse for you." I stood up and Dom did the same.

"I'm going on a business trip to Vegas in a couple weeks. I was wondering if you wanted to go with me. I figured it could be a start since we haven't been anywhere together in almost a year. I can rent our favorite room at the MGM and stay two extra days."

I thought I about it. I figured it would be a good start. While Dom was in meetings, I could take his debit card and go shopping at the outlets and get a two-hour massage.

"I guess so, if everything works out at the clinic." I smirked.

Dom hugged me and chuckled. "I know I ain't got shit to worry about, my dick clean. I ain't never fuck Monee without a condom, I promise you that," he said with confidence.

After dinner, Dom walked me to his truck and then walked into his mother's house. I drove back to the hills with so much on my mind. I was looking forward to what the next couple weeks had in store for me. I knew with me and Dom trying to work things out, shit was going to be crazy.

When I got home, it was quiet. I turned on every light and got comfortable. I poured a glass of wine and began walking around my home. It was a four-bedroom family home, and only me and Dom lived in it. We bought our dream home knowing we would raise our kids in it. So we didn't start off small until we had kids, we wanted to already be prepared. I walked into each room, thinking about the children I wanted to have. I wanted all boys and surprisingly Dom wanted all girls. I smiled at the thought of all the conversations we had about children. But then I thought about the birth control that was sitting on my uterus. When I first found out Dom was cheating, I wasted no time stopping my eggs. I wasn't in the business of being a baby mama. So I stopped trying to conceive.

That was two years ago.

I sipped my wine and headed back down the stairs. My house was so lonely. For the first time in months, I wished Dom was home, and was kind of glad he would be coming home, even though he would be living in our backyard where the guesthouse was…

Vindictive

Monee

Two weeks later…

It had been two weeks, and I was still pissed off at Dom and Shanay's ass. I couldn't believe I had to fight this bitch and now it was all over social media, still, after *two long weeks*. My job was sweating me, talking about letting me go, and they were pressing this lawsuit even though Dom was the one that told Shanay. My job claimed I still breached my contract and other girls in the club were airing out their married clients and quitting their jobs. I was accused of starting drama and causing the club a lot of money. It was all just a fucking mess. I didn't have money and I damn sure couldn't lose my job, but my boss already told me I had one more week to work. I needed Dom's ass handled just so I could get some revenge. It was his fucking fault me and Shanay was fighting, so he was going to have to pay with blood, since he was trying to ruin my life and take all my money that I didn't even have.

Days later, I ended up in Watts at my brother Ravell's house. He lived in Nickerson Gardens and his specialty was robbing, banging, and killing. Dom thought he was hard because he was from The Bay. But he ain't have nothing on my brother. He was a goon.

After he let me in, we walked into his kitchen and he continued his routine. Counting money, and separating pills for his sales for the day. He had Roddy Rich blaring through his speakers like he was in the club. I was sure the whole project complex could hear his music.

I sat there watching him count hundred after hundred. My brother had always been a money making motherfucker. He dropped out of school at thirteen to provide for us, and had thousands ever since. You would have thought he had done more with his money, but he didn't. He had a slew of kids, and a bunch of homies in jail, so his money went to providing for everybody in the hood. I didn't understand it, but he was a grown man and was providing so I never said anything.

I stood up and turned down his music a little bit after we finished off our first blunt.

"So what brings you to the projects this early? You need some money or somebody messing with you?" he asked as he stuffed pills in a small zip-lock bag.

"Actually, I came to offer you some money, and yes somebody is fucking with me."

My brother stopped what he was doing and raised his eyebrow. "What you talking about, girl?"

"This baller nigga I been fucking with been hitting on me, like beating my ass. I been on the run from him for weeks but he won't leave me alone. So I was wondering if you could handle this pretty ass nigga," I lied. I knew my brother well. He was a dog and didn't care about his baby mama, and he was the biggest hoe in the projects. I knew he would laugh if I told him why I was feuding with Dom. So I had to add some extras. I didn't give a fuck.

"Oh, word? Where this bitch nigga live at? You know I don't play that domestic violence shit," my brother stated, fully interested in my plan.

"He live up in the hill. I got his address and his work address." I reached in my pocket and pulled out a piece of paper with all his info. I handed it to my brother.

He looked at it and smirked. "This will be easy, I know that area. Police hardly up there. I'll catch that nigga slippin', and move in on his ass."

I nodded my head. "Thank you, bro. I'm just ready for this nigga to leave me alone. Here is three-grand up front. I'll give you the rest when it's done and over." I slid him three bands, but he gave me a rack back.

"I don't need all that. When it's over, just shoot me another two grand, and we good."

We shook hands.

After smoking one more blunt with my brother, I was ready to start my day. It felt good knowing Dom's ass was going to be handled, and hopefully come up dead on the news…

Caught slipping

Dom

After finally getting Shanay to talk to me and my mom, I felt relieved. I was looking forward to our mini getaway to Las Vegas to ball out and get back connected. I knew she wasn't fully there with me and probably was just horny like I was. But I was taking whatever she was giving me because I wanted my wife back on track with me. I was done with my old ways and I wanted my wife to understand that so we could get back on track. I missed her and I wanted nothing to do with Monee or any other woman. I had learned my lesson the hard way, now I was ready to man up and be a husband. I was in my thirties now and wanted to have sons, so I knew I had to set a good example for them by cleaning my act up before they were even born.

ROBIN

I walked out my office around seven in the evening like I always did. I was excited to leave work because after two weeks, Shanay was letting me come back in the house after sleeping in the guesthouse. But I was to sleep in the guest room now until we worked out our marriage. I had gotten a clean bill of health from my doctor earlier that day, so our Vegas trip was still on for the weekend. I got in my car and hit the freeway.

As I rode listening to music, I felt a little uneasy. I looked in my mirror and saw someone riding behind me. I kept my eyes on the car the whole time. It seemed as though they were following me, so I checked under my seat for my gun. I never left the house without it, especially since I had been staying in the hood at my mother's house. I still had it tucked and I was waiting to use it.

I got off at my exit and headed towards my house. I looked in my mirrors again and I didn't see the car anymore. I finally pulled in my driveway and killed my engine. I looked out the window and saw my Lamborghini truck. It was dirty and I could tell Shanay had been driving it all over town by the look of the dirty tires. I shook my head but figured it could have been worse with the way I had been toying around with her feelings.

I opened my car door but before I could step out, I felt a gun to my head.

"Get the fuck out the car, nigga," the man said. I smirked and stepped out like he asked.

"Where the money at, nigga?"

"I ain't got no money on me, bro, just credit cards," I said nonchalantly. I didn't know who this cat was but he had another thing coming if he didn't think I was waiting for him to slip up so I could blast his ass.

"Well let's go to the ATM then!" This nigga was serious, but I laughed.

"Yeah, right. You might as well kill me." I stepped back and looked at his gun as he tried to pull the trigger. His damn gun was on safety…

"You trying to rob a nigga with the safety on ya gun? You must be amateur, nigga," I said as I took my gun from my waist and pointed at his forehead.

"Drop the muthafuckin' gun, nigga, and lay down on the ground," I snarled at him. I figured he was shocked I had a gun in my waist while wearing a two-thousand-dollar suit while driving a Mercedes. His eyes grew big like he had seen a ghost or ran into the police.

Dude laid on the ground with his legs and arms spread. I kicked his gun to the side so he wouldn't try and grab it. I kneeled down and looked at the dude. I didn't know who he was, but I wanted to find out. I kept the barrel of my gun to his forehead. I was ready to kill this nigga. I had been robbed before, and I promised I'd never get caught slipping again. My gun was legal and he was on my property.

I had a license to kill.

"Who the fuck sent you, nigga?" I gritted at him as I smashed his face into the cold pavement.

"Fuck you, nigga, I'm not telling you!" he shouted.

"Ohhh, you want to die tonight, huh?" I hit him in the mouth with my pistol.

Dude started spitting blood. "Kill me, nigga. I'm never a snitch!"

I smirked. "Aight…" I took my nine and let off two shots into both his legs. I decided not to kill him, thinking about all the legal shit I'd have to go through before they could prove my innocence. The gunshot and the sound of the man screaming from the burning in his calves sent Shanay running out the house.

"Oh my god, Dominic, what happened?!" she shouted.

"Go call the cops. Somebody set me up. He tried to rob me, so I shot him," I said calmly, trying not to scare Shanay, but it was already too late. She stood there gawking at the screaming man with her hands over her mouth. I snapped.

"Go do what the fuck I said, Shanay, NOOWWW," I roared at her, startling her.

She ran back into the house and did as she was told as I paced my driveway. I saw my nosey ass white neighbors coming outside. They probably were waiting for some nigga shit to pop off at my house the way they stared at us every day, and now they had it. I had a screaming grown man in my driveway at gunpoint and he was bleeding profusely. I was angry and wanted to know who set me up, but this nigga wasn't talking.

After the cops hauled the man off to the hospital, I spoke with a detective. After telling me they would start an investigation and call me if anything came up, they left. I looked at the detective's card and then slipped it in my pocket. I then went in the house to calm Shanay down. It was hard but eventually after a couple blunts and some wine, she was off to sleep and ready for our ride to Vegas the following morning…

Vegas

Shanay

It was me and Dom's second day in Vegas and I was feeling relaxed. I had been shopping and had at least four different massages. I was so tense when I first got here after Dom almost getting robbed in front of our home. I had never seen so much blood. But when I found out Dom had only shot him in the calves, it soothed me a little, knowing he hadn't killed anyone. The situation was still crazy and didn't make sense to me. Dom had been robbed in the past at a liquor store by his mother's. I could admit, Dom was a bit flashy, especially when it came to cars. He always had the attention on him even when he didn't try. However, this set up felt different. Only a handful of people knew where we lived, and the guy on the ground looked so familiar. I stood on our balcony in our penthouse suite looking out at the strip in deep thought. That's when it hit me. I began choking on my THC pen and ran into my room.

"That bitch Monee, that was her fucking brother," I muttered as I went and got my phone off the charger.

It was six in the evening and I was tipsy. I had time for this bitch Monee and I was going to let her know I was on to her grimy ass. I quickly pushed her name in my iPhone and surprisingly, the bitch answered on the first ring.

"What you want, bitch? Calling to kiss my ass?" she stated in such a cocky tone.

"You wish, bitch. You sent your ugly ass, slow ass brother to my house to try and rob Dom. Well, guess what bitch, he failed, his gun was on safety when he tried to pull the trigger, and his ass ended up on the other end of the gun. Pull some shit like that again, Monee, and I'll fuck you up again, even worse, hoe. Find somebody else nigga to be mad at, you broke ass bitch!" I shouted through the phone, kind of laughing at the fact that her brother was really dumb. I had known him for years. He repeated each grade two times until he was twenty-two years old. She must have been as dumb as him sending him to rob Dom with a gun on safety.

"Bitch, I ain't got shit to do with nothing, so don't be throwing my name in shit. I don't give a fuck about you or Dom. I'm living my life happy, unlike you. You can't even fuck your man correctly, bitch. Don't forget why he came running to me and you did too. Have a nice life with Dom's wack ass, bitch. I know he will be cheating on you soon, good day." The call dismissed.

This bitch had me fucked up if she thought she was just going to hang up in my face. I called her phone back to back until she finally turned it off.

ME: Fucking Biiiittttcchhh, I'll fuck you up Monee. Try and rob me bitch, you gonna end up dead. You

*better remember who the harder friend was,
ALWAYS. I was the gangsta, you was the HOE,
remember that!*

I sent her that text and finished off my half a bottle
of wine.

By the time Dom stepped in the room, I was filthy
drunk. I ended up ordering a bottle of champagne
and Hennessey. I didn't even realize I had been
drinking for an hour.

"Nay, are you drunk?" Dom asked in a confused
tone as he took off his dress shirt and tie.

I stood from the table and wobbled over to him,
trying to look sexy. But the way he was looking at
me, clearly I was looking a mess.

"Yes! Dominic, I'm drunk. And it's all you and
Monee's fault!" I blurted out and threw myself on
him. Dom wrapped his arms around me.

"Woman, we're supposed to be going out with my co-workers and you are trashed. Maybe you need to lay down for a couple hours. We can skip the strip and you can sleep this off." Dom walked me over to the bed.

"No, I want to fuck! Fuck me now!!! Isn't that what you like? Ain't that why you cheated because we wasn't fucking?" I started unbuttoning his pants and they fell to the floor. I started massaging his dick, making it rise.

"Nay, you drunk, I can't fuck you like this," Dom uttered, but I knew he wanted it. His dick was telling me otherwise the way it aroused in my hand.

"You're my husband. You can fuck me in public if you want." I dropped to my knees and pulled his aching arousal from his boxer briefs. I took his ten inches and took it to the back of my throat. I gagged a little but I kept going. Dom grunted from the feeling and looked down at me in shock. I guess he couldn't believe how I was taking his dick so far back. I learned to just breathe through my nose and it worked out well.

"Damn, Shanay, I thought you wanted me to fuck you," Dom said as he watched me continue to take him in my mouth. I stood up and pushed him on the bed. I was already naked under my robe so I climbed on top of him and slid down on his stick. I moaned as I glided his dick inside of me, causing me to become extremely wet. It didn't hurt, and I was gaining some weight, so it felt so right.

I started kissing Dom on his neck and lips while he thrusted me from under. The sound of my juices flowing as he stroked me had me going wild. For once I didn't have to use lubricant and I wasn't complaining about him being too big. We started kissing passionately as I came over and over on his stick.

"You're mine, Dominic, and I don't want no other female to have you. I love you, and I hope you won't step out on me again," I softly whispered in his ear.

"I love you too, Nay, and I will never step out on you again."

Dom began thrusting me hard and fast. I moaned loudly as he continued to stroke me fast. He then switched our position and put me in doggystyle. It had been a while since I had that but I took it like a gangsta. I let Dom smack my ass and give me deep strokes. I knew he was happy his wife was finally being submissive to him. I vowed I'd never leave my husband hanging in any aspect of our relationship again. I was going to have his back just like he had mine.

Dom came inside of me and then collapsed on the side of me. I could feel myself sobering up from the sweaty sex we just had.

"I think I can go out on the strip now. Let me shower and eat some bread." I climbed out of bed.

As I showered, I heard Dom sneak in. "If you are looking for round two, I'm all out, playboy." We both laughed.

"Nah, not even, I just wanted to shower with you."

As Dom washed my body, I decided to tell him about Monee. I knew for a fact that was her brother and she had something to do with it.

"Dom, I got into it with Monee today. It was her brother that robbed you. I recognized his face."

Dom stopped washing me and then turned me around. "Why didn't you tell me that sooner, Monee?" He frowned.

"Because, it just hit me today when I was drinking, Dom. Had I known at the scene, I would have told the cops."

Dom slammed his fist into his hand. "I'm going to kill that bitch," he gritted in anger.

"As much as I want her dead, I think we need to let the police handle this. You are going to have to get a restraining order on her if she is doing stuff like this. I've known her for a long time, and when she is mad, she is devious."

Dom sighed. "When we get back to Los Angeles, we are making a lot of changes. That bitch is going down."

"Well, for now, let's just enjoy our vacation before we have to think about our reality."

Me and Dom got dressed and went to enjoy a high class night on the town…

$$$$$

Two days later, we were back home. We couldn't even soak in the wonderful vacation we were just on. We had to talk to the detective, and book a marriage counselor. Dom went and got a restraining order on Monee and we got a new security system. I wasn't taking any chances with that bitch Monee

because I knew shit was going to hit the fan once
she found out Dom put that restraining order on her.

I'll handle Dom

Three days later…

Monee

I stood in my brother's room at his baby mother's house looking at him while shaking my head. I was so pissed, I didn't know how to react. I didn't know what had happened, but all I knew, Dom's ass was still alive and well while my life was crumbling. That shit wasn't sitting well with me, so I had to come with a different plan since my brother couldn't get it done. Dom had sent me a fucking restraining order, now I was hearing detectives wanted to talk to me about the attempted robbery case my brother was going through. I wasn't answering to nobody, so I was in and out of everywhere I went with the quickness.

"How the fuck did you forget the safety, Ravell? That was the first thing you supposed to do is take the gun off safety before you even got out the car. I swear, I should have done it myself, Ravell. I'm not paying you shit!" I shouted.

"What?! This was your idea, Monee, don't try and leave me hanging. I got court fees, I gotta pay my bail, and they trying to give a nigga life because I already got two strikes. If you don't give me my money, I'm going to rat your scandalous ass to the cops, Monee. You can pull that fuck shit with these trick niggas, but not me," my brother roared.

"You ain't telling nobody, shit! You already committed the crime and you still going to jail. So telling on me ain't gonna change nothing. I'll do my time, nigga. I need to sit down anyway," I admitted.

As much as I hated jail, I could feel my life moving in that direction. I had been to jail for violence numerous times, and I felt that side of me coming out. I hated it, but every time I came out of jail, I went straight, for a while… but if I was to happen to go to jail over this situation, it was going to be my lesson.

"Whatever, Monee, you ain't shit! Get the fuck out my house." I grabbed my purse and then turned on my heels.

"Oh, let me fluff your pillow for you." I smiled as I walked over to his bed.

"Get out, Monee, don't try and butter me up."

At that moment, I slipped a pillow from under him, catching him off guard. Before he could say anything, I smushed the pillow over his face and started suffocating him. My brother had me fucked up if he thought I was going to let him get away with snitching on me. He was the biggest no snitching advocate, talking about turning me in. He had to go…

He tried to kick his way out the situation but his legs were in pain, and his arms were becoming weak from the pressure I applied on his face. I watched his body become weak and then he finally stopped moving. I removed the pillow from his face and his eyes were popped out and his light complexion was blue. I closed his eyes and then gazed at his dead body.

"I thought you knew, snitches get stitches." I shook my head and exited the room.

"Alright Renee, I'm out," I said to his baby mother, who was slaving over the stove for a dead man.

"Alright, Monee, thanks for stopping by." She waved, and I headed out to my car. I knew his baby mama was going to be sad when she saw his dead body, but I knew she would eventually get over it. My brother was a dog to her, and she always wished death on him. Now her wish had come true.

I skirted out the projects with my music blasting. I headed back to my new condo and put my next plan into motion. It was time to get Dom's dog ass…

$$$$$

One Week Later…

I had been following Shanay and Dom all week. I was becoming obsessed with how happy they were trying to showcase. If Shanay was satisfying Dom, it was because of me. Now he wanted me cut off like I never existed, like he never started this shit.

I watched them go to the mall, I watched him take her to the dealership for a Maserati truck. I watched them go to dinner, and just live it the fuck up while everybody had their hands in my pockets.

"Bitch ass nigga," I said as I watched him help Shanay pack up her new truck. It looked like she was going on vacation alone and she was glowing. I wondered if the bitch was pregnant the way she was glowing.

I sat back and smoked my blunt, mad as hell. I watched them kiss passionately before Shanay jumped in her driver seat and pulled out her driveway.

"Call me when you pick up your sister or when you get on the road," I heard Dom shout down his driveway. I slid down in my seat and watched her drive off. Once I slid back up, Dom was back in the house.

I waited until late night to put my plan in motion. Clearly Dom was quick on his feet when he was alert, so I wanted to catch him off guard, and unarmed. I didn't even know Dom rode around with a gun, but I was sure he didn't sleep with one under his pillow…

It was two in the morning when I woke up behind the wheel of my car. After finally getting my mind together, I remembered where I was. In front of Dom's home, seeking revenge. I still had the same energy before I had fallen asleep, so I grabbed my gun and headed up to his driveway. All the lights were off in the home, so I knew he had to be in a deep sleep. I walked up his long driveway to their door. When I got to the door, I reached in my pocket for a single key. Shanay was so stupid. She had given me a key and code to her alarm system when she first moved in her home.

"Stupid bitch," I thought to myself as I unlocked the door. I quickly walked in and to my surprise, the alarm system wasn't on. It beeped as though it was off. When I walked in, I took my small flashlight from my back pocket and started tip-toeing around their living room. I looked at all their pictures and all their awards from work. Shanay was smart and so was Dom. They took the white man's way out the hood, and I wished I had done the same. I had fucked off everything I touched, including my scholarship to USC.

Right when I was about to graduate high school, I got into a brawl in my advanced math class. Things got so crazy, I knocked out our sixty-year-old teacher. They were ready to get rid of my ass. I was handed my high school diploma, but my scholarship was snatched from under me. Ever since then, I had been stripping and having sex for money while Shanay went on with her life to college. I know I had told Shanay I didn't consider her a friend, but I did. She had been my only friend that didn't judge me for my lifestyle and I loved that about her. That's why my animosity was really geared at Dom. I still loved Shanay as a best friend deep down inside.

I became irritated and remembered what I came to do. However, before I could even get to the stairs, gunshots started flying. I was so scared I dropped my gun. But I felt hot shells hitting my body causing me to fall. I felt a bullet hit my chest, my shoulder and my stomach, and in my neck… the rest hit the walls. I laid on the ground, wounded, wondering what had happened. That's when I saw the light, but it was only Dom turning on the living room light.

"Monee, what the fuck, man! I thought you were an intruder, I thought you were somebody else!" Dom shouted. I saw him pacing as I held onto the little life I had in me.

"You came here to try and kill me?!" he shouted. I assumed he had seen my gun.

"I'm sorry, Dominic, I loved you. But you hurt me…" were my last words before I blacked out…

It was an accident

Dom

I rushed through the hospital as they wheeled Monee to the operating room. I swear on my life, I didn't know she was in my living room. I hated Monee, but deep down, I knew she was still Shanay's best friend even though they were mad. I would never kill her on purpose. Had I known it was her, I would have wrestled her down to the ground and took her gun. She was a hard target to stop and I could have taken a gunshot wound if she shot me. I was so tired but I heard somebody come in my home and I knew it wasn't Shanay. I was so deprived of sleep from working a twenty-four-hour shift to meet a deadline, I started shooting. Not to mention, I had forgotten to turn on our security system. I was so stressed out, so I didn't take the time to think Monee would actually come in my house and try to kill me.

After I showed the cops what our home cameras showed, they didn't lock me up, and I followed them to the hospital. I called Shanay back to back until she answered. Shanay had gone on vacation with her sister so I could have the house to myself to rest. I told her she should have stayed but she insisted on leaving, now I wished she would have just stayed home.

"Hellooo, what's up, Dom? Is everything okay?" Shanay shouted through the phone. I could tell she was in the club having a good time. Her and her sister had only driven to Palm Springs.

"Nay, you gotta come back. Monee broke in and was going to kill me. I thought she was a real intruder or had sent someone else again. But it was her. So I shot her. She is in a coma. I'm at the hospital now," I was speaking quickly.

"Oh my god, are you serious? Stay put, I'm on my way!" Shanay shouted through the phone.

As I sat in the lobby waiting, numerous cops and detectives came and talked to me. I told them everything that had been going on, and they already had the robbery on file from her brother. I had a restraining order on Monee, so she was not to be in my home. The police continued to pressure me to go down to the station, but I told them my lawyer was on his way to the hospital and I was staying put. Once my lawyer came with all the paperwork I needed, the cops cleared out.

"Alright, Mr. Thomas, you stay up. I'll be at your home first thing in the morning before reporters show, so try and get a good night's rest. Don't stay in this hospital all night. The girl is a vegetable," my lawyer stated as he walked out of the hospital. I flopped on one of the chairs in the waiting room and waited for Shanay to show. I found myself dozing off, but I was awakened by Shanay's screams.

"No!" she shouted. I opened my eyes and jumped up. She was trying to attack the doctors and nurses that were caring for Monee while her sister held her back.

"She can't be, she just can't be!" she shouted.

We locked eyes. I could see the anger in her eyes as she gazed at me like a pit bull. I knew she would be mad, Monee was her best friend. She had known her longer than me, and they had ties.

"This is all your fault! Had you kept your dick in your pants, none of this would have happened!" Shanay ran to me and started pounding me with her fists as she cried out. I grabbed her in a tight bearhug, trying to calm her down.

"Shanay, I'm so sorry, I didn't mean for all this to happen," I said in her ear as I held her.

"You did this, Dominic, you!" She broke away from my hold and stormed out of the hospital.

"Dom, she is really hurt. You might want to give her a few days before you approach her," her sister said, and then she ran out the hospital behind her sister. I wanted to go run out with her. Maybe run out and get hit by a car. I felt like shit, and there was nothing I could do about it. I had killed my wife's best friend…

Epilogue

Shanay

One year later…

Even after everything, I was still a wreck over losing Monee, but I held my head up high and moved on with my life. I never thought in a million years she would be dead by the hands of my husband. I believed him when he said it was an accident, so we went through heavy counseling to get back on track. I had shut down completely, even moving out of me and Dom's house we shared together. I just couldn't live there. Not with my best friend's blood staining my carpet.

I sat in my boy Juno's tattoo shop, vibing to "Chase the Bag" by Roddy Rich. The clear sounds and bass threw me into a zone as I sipped my Hennessy Juno had given me. He was tatting my back with

Monee's name decked out with falling dollars. It was my first tattoo and I felt this was a chapter in my life I didn't want to forget.

"If it hurts too bad, let me know," I heard Juno say as he wiped what he had done so far with cooling aloe.

"Nope, I'm good. I've felt worse pain in my heart," I said as I continued to sip. He then passed me his blunt and I hit it a couple times and passed it to him. Juno hit it a couple times as well and then got back to work.

"That shit dope," I heard Dom say from behind me to Juno. He had walked in while I was getting tatted.

Although me and Dom were going to counseling twice a week, we did most of it online. So we didn't see each other much and I was living in a condo on Sunset Blvd. I decided to invite him to my tatt session, so we could talk outside of counseling. I was slowly getting better. I was having thoughts of coming home now that I was opening up to him. My mother and his mother were my saints. They were rooting for me in every angle and assured me it wasn't my fault and I could move on with Dom if that was what God was telling me to do. He had truly cleaned up his act and had convinced me finally.

"Thank you, I felt it was the right thing to do," I said as I tried to look up and give him a smile.

"I'll let you two talk in private. I'm going to go next door and get some food. Y'all want something?" Juno asked.

"Nah, I'm good," I said, and Dom declined as well.

When Juno walked out, Dom sat in his seat. He sat there quiet for a second, fidgeting with his phone until he noticed I wasn't doing the same. He stuffed his phone in his pocket and pierced his eyes on me.

"So, what's going on? How do you feel?" he asked.

"I'm doing well. I've been taking it one day at a time like our counselor told us. I'm finally feeling like myself again, that's why I came out and got my first tattoo." I smiled.

"Yeah, I see you, hardbody. You never wanted to get tatted with me. But I'm glad you are doing good. I miss the old you."

He was right. Dom was tatted from his neck to his waist, and I watched him get them all. He wanted me to get his name so bad, and I always told him no. I didn't want to damage my skin, but I felt like I owed Monee this tattoo. As much as we were beefing, I knew she always had my back in the worst times in my life. I blamed Dom more for what had happened than Monee. She was only doing her job while Dom was out satisfying his own needs. But now I felt like we had both grown from the dark place we were in, and I was moving forward with life.

"I miss the old me too, and she is back. So I've done a lot of soul searching, and I realized that I am not complete without you. I want to move back in the house with you and start counseling every day together until we are comfortable enough to stop going."

Dom smiled. "I've been waiting to hear that for weeks. This last year has been hell for me, for the both of us, and I just want to get back on track. I've been going to church with my mother, asking God to forgive me for killing Monee, and cheating on you. I've had so many sleepless nights from all my demons, but lately, I've been sleeping. I think I've come to peace with everything, and I'm ready to move forward with you too."

"It feels good to hear you are doing well too, Dom. Your feelings and needs do matter and I've learned that." I stood up and grabbed his hand, making him stand as well.

We hugged for the first time in months and it felt good to have his arms around me. He was faithful and God fearing now, and I loved him for becoming a man, finally. At that moment, our hug turned into kissing. Dom grabbed my thighs and my ass and cuffed it in his hands.

"You got that ass back, I see. I like that," he said in a seductive tone. Dom hadn't lusted over me in so long, but it felt good.

"Yup, I gained 20 pounds in all the right places." I started kissing on his neck. I felt his manhood rising. I knew it had been a while for Dom, and I was ready to give it to him.

I broke away from Dom and locked Juno's door. I couldn't wait to get home, I had to have my husband at that moment. Me and Dom made love on the wall of Juno's office until Juno came back knocking. I knew from that moment me and Dom would have more spontaneous moments. I knew that would be one of the many things I'd love to do to keep our relationship tight.

After that day, me and Dom didn't have any more problems, he was faithful to me, and I was faithful to him… even another year later, I had our first daughter… we were happy.

the end.

Thanks for the support! Find me on all social media sites!

https://www.facebook.com/RobinChartay/

e-mail me with your feedback
novelsbyauthorrobin@gmail.com

https://www.brandbulliesusa.com/author-robin

Find me on Instagram @_chartay_

BRAND BULLIES PUBLISHING PRESENTS
Young Black
BILLIONAIRES
A Classy Romance
ROBIN

Available on Amazon

When
A GANGSTA FALLS
IN
Love
ROBIN

www.ingramcontent.com/pod-product-compliance
Lightning Source LLC
Chambersburg PA
CBHW021955170726
47994CB00021B/505